MONSTER TRUCKS

by Anika Denise

Illustrated by Nate Wragg

HARPER
An Imprint of HarperCollinsPublishers

ISBN 978-0-06-234522-6 (trade bdg.)

The artist used acrylic paints and digital color to create the illustrations for this book.
Typography by Dana Fritts
18 19 20 SCP 10 9 8 7 6 5 4
❖
First Edition

For Screamie Michalak, Scara LaReau,
Kristen Creepy, and Emily Van Eeek!
—Anika Denise

For Crystal—your love and support
inspire me in every way, every day.
—Nate Wragg

On a SPOOKY speedway . . .

MONSTER TRUCKS MOAN!

MONSTER TRUCKS GRUMBLE!

MONSTER TRUCKS GROAN!

FRANKENTRUCK
is first to arrive.

With a jump of his cables,
HE'S ALIVE!
HE'S ALIVE!

WEREWOLF TRUCK
croons a gravelly tune.
First a *SCREECH,*
then a *GROWL*

and a HOWL
at the moon!

Next up: **ZOMBIE TRUCK!**

Headlights glow green. Dripping in diesel,

he's CRANKY and *MEAN!*

Then out of the shadows,
GHOST TRUCK appears,
rattling his axles and grinding his gears!

VAMPIRE TRUCK is *toothsome* and cruel.

He waits for his victims
and drinks down their fuel!

Up goes the flag!
Each rig takes his place—
ready to RUMBLE

in the
MONSTER TRUCK RACE!

On a **SMOKING** speedway . . .

MONSTER TRUCKS **TOW!**

MONSTER TRUCKS **REV!**

MONSTER TRUCKS **GO!!!**

When out of the pit . . . with a **PUTT** and a **TOOT**
comes a **LITTLE BLUE BUS,**
looking perky . . . and cute.

On a SMASH-'EM-UP-speedway . . .

MONSTER TRUCKS SNEER!

MONSTER TRUCKS SNICKER!

MONSTER TRUCKS **LEER!**

The CACKLING monsters
lick their chops for some LUNCH!

She's a MEAL ON WHEELS . . .
to this *FRIGHTENING* bunch.

"I'm not scared!" toots the LITTLE BLUE BUS.

"Hope you monsters are hungry—

you'll be *EATING MY DUST!*"

Over rugged terrain—
with a **HEAVE** and a **HO**

and a spin of her tires
and a **READY-SET-GO!**—

the LITTLE BLUE BUS
CHUG-CHUGS down the track.
She *buries* those monsters,
and she doesn't look back!

Then up from the rubble, one truck burns a trail.

He's **MAD**–and he's **THIRSTY** · · ·

and **HOT ON HER TAIL!**

But the LITTLE BLUE BUS
has a **TRICK** up her hood.
She **SLAMS** on her brakes
and **LOCKS** 'em up good!

SPUN OUT and SPUTTERING, he ROLLS to a stall.

Can you guess who's in front
when the checkered flags fall?

The LITTLE BLUE BUS!
She's got GUMPTION and PLUCK

we'll just call it . . . luck.